To Radley & Rhett,

Let your imagination soar!

Alexandra
Adlawan

## Dedication

Writing and illustrating books is harder than I thought and more rewarding than I could have ever imagined. None of this would have been possible without my friend and mentor, *Tawd B. Dorenfeld*. Many have encouraged me along the way, but Tawd guided me through all the ups and downs to help me achieve my vision of Maddie and Albert. He stands by me during every struggle and all my successes.

Tawd, your understanding and patience is very much appreciated and is a true example of friendship.

# Flying
# The Imaginary Skies

## THE ADVENTURES OF MADDIE AND ALBERT

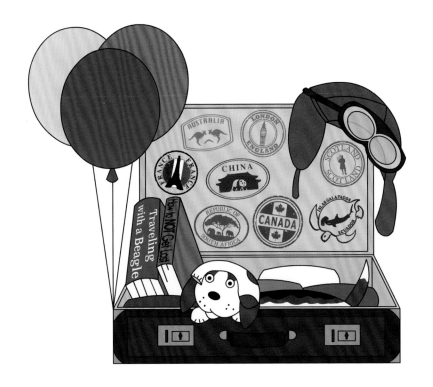

## WRITTEN AND ILLUSTRATED BY ALEXANDRA ADLAWAN

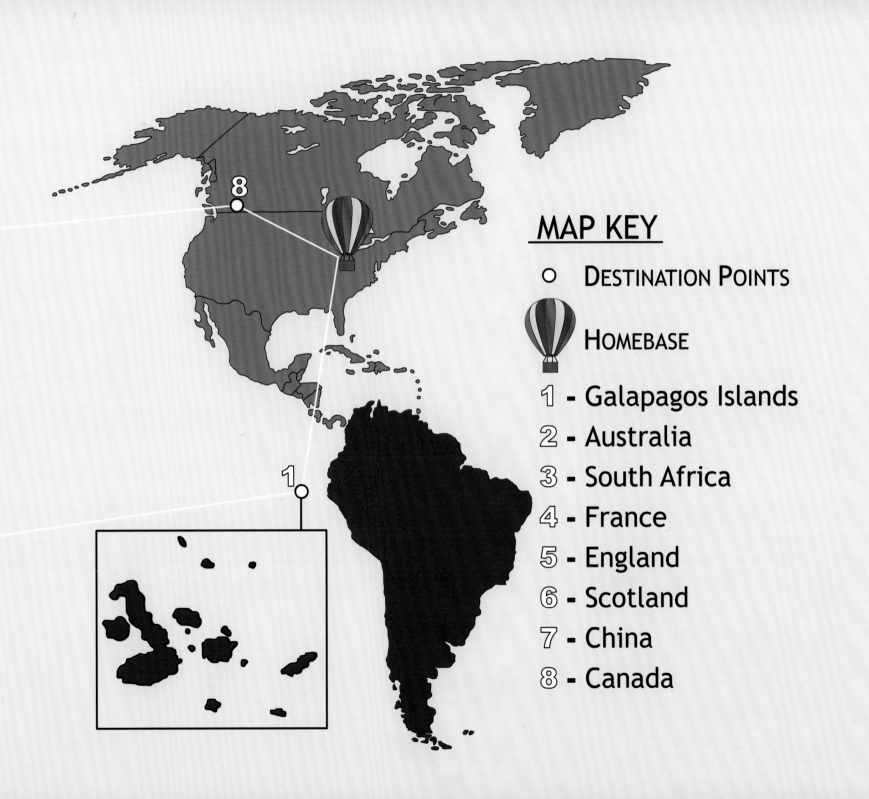

## MAP KEY

○ DESTINATION POINTS

🎈 HOMEBASE

**1** - Galapagos Islands
**2** - Australia
**3** - South Africa
**4** - France
**5** - England
**6** - Scotland
**7** - China
**8** - Canada

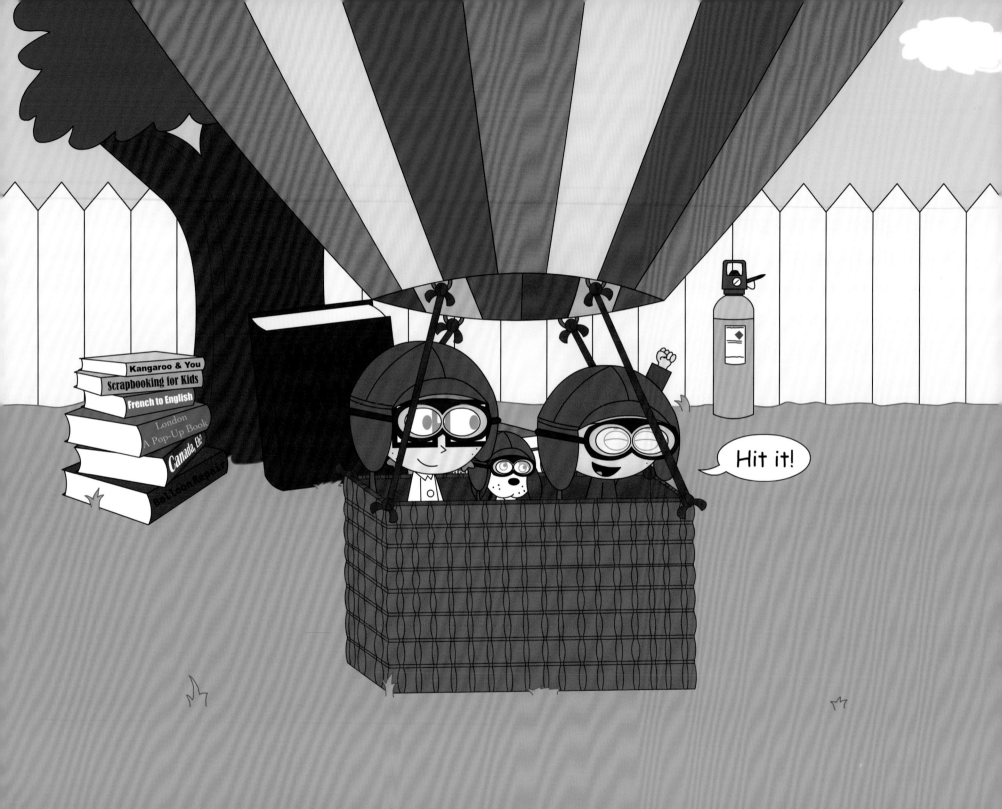

# The Galapagos Islands

A – We're here on Isabela Island, one of the main 13 islands of the Galapagos. On Urbina Bay, we found many land iguanas and a friendly giant tortoise.

M – I've found my spirit animal! The blue-footed booby! Look at his cute little waddle!

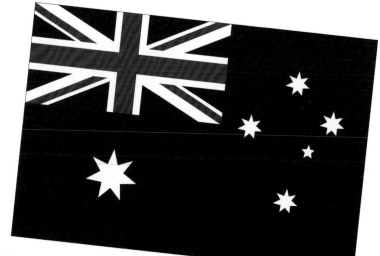

A – While bringing a koala back to his home, a kangaroo gave us a lift. Houdini snuck into the mother's pouch when the kangaroo joey got out. During the trip we passed Uluru, a massive block of sandstone that is sacred to indigenous Australians.

M – Today, Albert proved that it is possible to get motion sickness from riding a kangaroo.

# South Africa

A – While in South Africa, we took a safari in Kruger National Park, one of the largest national parks in the world, with a diverse landscape full of animals. Maddie and I went out to search for the Big Five, the hardest animals to find on safari. But luckily we found one of each all hanging out together.

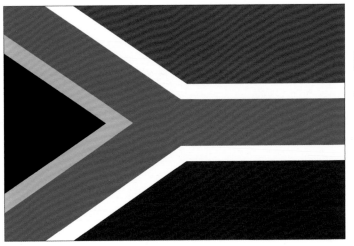

M – Albert got to ride a rhino, Houdini made a new friend, and I hugged a lion! Best day ever!

M – I'm really enjoying the French cuisine, especially the chocolate croissants. Albert has really taken to the way of the mime. He hasn't spoken in 3 hours and it's starting to get a little creepy.

A – While in Paris we visited the Eiffel Tower. It was built for the 1889 World's Fair and has become one of the most recognizable structures in the world. I tried to tell Maddie this through mime but I don't think she understood.

# England

A - I wanted to visit Big Ben and the Tower of London, but Maddie insisted on pestering the guards at Buckingham Palace.

M - That guard was one tough nut to crack. His mouth twitched a bit, so I call that a victory for us.

# SCOTLAND

M — I really wanted to meet the Loch Ness Monster. Albert thought playing "Scotland the Brave" on the bagpipes might draw Nessie out of hiding. But with the way Albert was playing, Nessie is probably long gone.

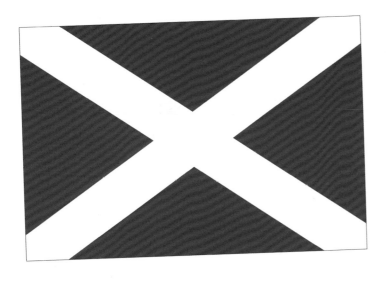

A — I don't care what Maddie and Houdini think — I rocked that bagpipe!

A – The Great Wall of China is the longest structure ever built by humans, and contrary to popular belief, you cannot see it from space.

M – With its long walkways, the Great Wall of China is the perfect place to fly a kite!

# CANADA

A – While visiting Crowsnest Pass in Alberta, we came across some Mounties on patrol. They treated us to a pancake breakfast. The smell of the flapjacks attracted a beaver, who stole mine when I wasn't looking.

M – Best maple syrup I've ever tasted! I drank it straight from the jug!

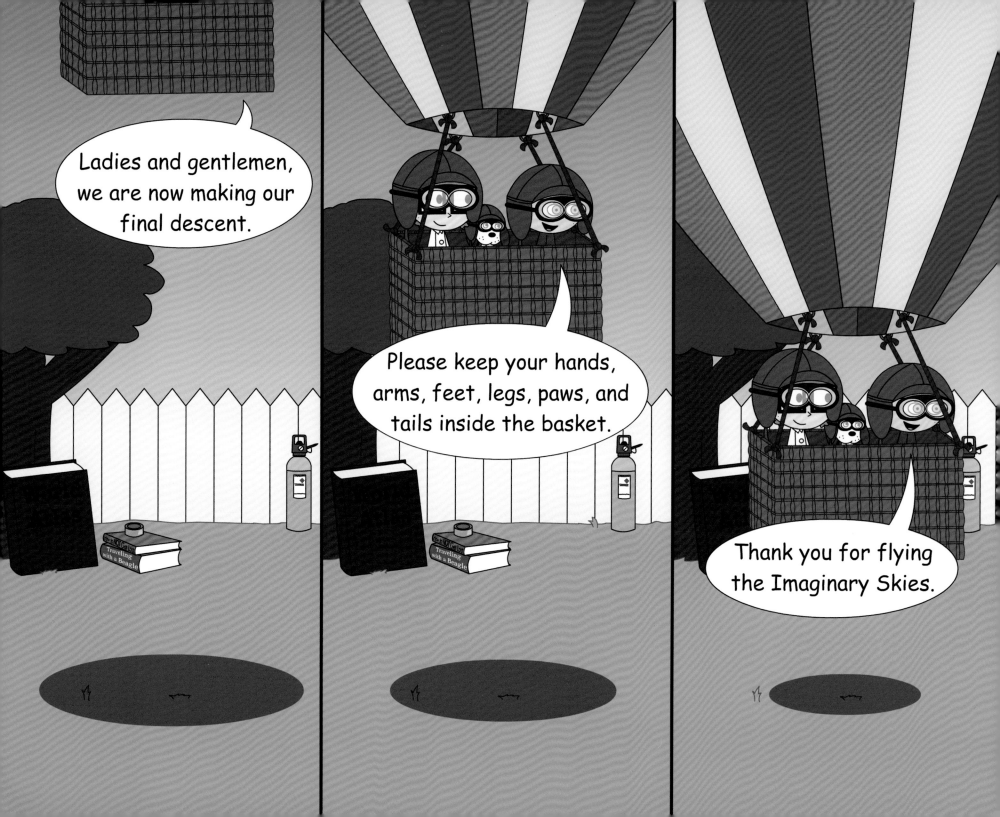

# Author's Note

There were many inspirations that came together to create FLYING THE IMAGINARY SKIES. At first, I was inspired to create greeting cards based on countries around the world. That turned into a calendar for my mom and in the end it only made sense to turn the whole idea into the third book in THE ADVENTURES OF MADDIE AND ALBERT series.

Having a mom who works for a major airline exposed me to traveling at the young age of six months, on my first trip to Canton, Ohio. As you can see from the photos on this page, I have visited a few of the destinations that Maddie and Albert travel to. I am so thankful to my mom and dad for always taking me on endless adventures.

For the record, the distance between Canton, Ohio and the Galapagos Islands really is 2,916 miles.

# About the Author

Alexandra Adlawan was born and raised in Long Beach, California. Despite the challenges of being diagnosed with Autism Spectrum Disorder, writing and illustrating has been the one constant in her life. The stories of Maddie and Albert are about encouraging the imagination within young people and embracing the differences in others.

## More From
## THE ADVENTURES OF MADDIE AND ALBERT

Maddie is mischievous, daring, and witty. Albert is intelligent, rational, and sharp-witted.
Who would have thought two total opposites could be the best of friends? But with his brains and her imagination, they are the perfect team.

With Maddie's ability to come up with crazy things to do and Albert's willingness to go along with anything, the fun this summer is guaranteed. Join these two best friends to see what adventures they have planned for their vacation.

REVIEW: "I've been offered a lot of children's books during my time at the big brick and mortar bookstore and yours is not only beautifully written and illustrated but delivers a wonderful message on many levels. I look forward to more adventures with Maddie and Albert." Diane Sands, Advocate & Consultant

REVIEW: "Kids will love the ongoing adventures of Maddie and Albert – who wouldn't get the giggles at the antics of these two best friends?" Sally J. Pla, author or the 2018 Dolly Gray Children's Literature Award for *The Someday Birds*

Amazing Artists LLC

Visit our Website: www.AmazingArtists.Online

Follow us on Facebook: www.Facebook.com/AlexandraAdlawanArtist

*Across the Spectrum*

ISBN 9781732446243

Library of Congress
Control Number: 2020901152

Printed and Bounded in China

Published by:
**Amazing Artists LLC**
Long Beach, CA USA
www.AmazingArtists.Online